KAARINA
and the Sugar Bag Vest

KAARINA
and the Sugar Bag Vest

IRMA McDONOUGH MILNES

illustrated by
SAMI SUOMALAINEN

ANNICK PRESS LTD.
Toronto • New York

Annick Press gratefully acknowledges the support of the Canada
Council and the Ontario Arts Council.

Canadian Cataloguing in Publication Data

McDonough, Irma, 1924-
  Kaarina and the sugar bag vest

(Annick window on the world books)
ISBN 1-55037-356-0

I. Suomalainen, Sami. II. Title. III. Series.

PS8575.D65K33 1994   jC813'.54   C94-930607-X
PZ7.M55Ka 1994

Distributed in Canada by:
Firefly Books Ltd.
250 Sparks Ave.
Willowdale, ON M2H 2S4

Published in the U.S.A. by Annick Press (U.S.) Ltd.
Distributed in the U.S.A. by:
Firefly Books Ltd.
P.O. Box 1325
Ellicott Station
Buffalo, NY 14205

Printed and bound in Canada by
Quebecor Printing

For Dale and Kaija,
with love

CONTENTS

Winter Underwear

I am Mother's first-born child. She named me
Kaarina after her favourite sister. It's a Finnish
name.

My brother is younger than I am. We call him
The Boy because he's the only boy in the family. I'm
the only girl.

The Boy doesn't like being second. There is a
good reason. Mother says we should not waste
anything – including winter underwear. So when I
grow out of my long johns, Mother fixes them for
The Boy. She opens up the seams down the front so
that he can pee without sliding the long johns down
his legs, like I have to.

But The Boy says he's the only boy in his class
who has to wear his sister's hand-me-downs. The
other boys laugh at him in the lavatory, and The Boy
doesn't like that at all.

He isn't the only one who has to wear funny

underwear in the winter, though. Mother sews cotton vests for me. They are made from sugar bags. The bags hold 100 pounds of sugar and they have bright red and blue lettering on them. Dad brings them home from the co-op store where he works.

One of the vests says 100% PURE CANE SUGAR in big red letters, right on the front, because sometimes the dye in the letters won't come out. Even if Mother boils the bags in lye for half a day.

But when I protest and refuse to wear that one, Mother hugs me and says that it just proves how sweet I am – "One hundred per cent is the sweetest anyone can be." But I never take my sweater off in front of anybody but the family. I don't want people to laugh at me.

At Aura's Office

My real name is Kaarina, but I have other names, too. The children at school call me Chipso, like the soap, maybe because my last name is Laakso, and that sounds a bit like Lux soap. But that's not funny enough, so Chipso it is – the soap that washes the Finns clean.

Then Aura, the cashier at the co-op, calls me Sunshine. I don't know why.

I go to see her often. She mostly lets me use "the tools of her trade." I press the rubber stamp on my school books; it says Workers' Co-operative Ltd. Then I try the typewriter. I know how to type my name.

Most of the people who work in the store are Finns and Ukrainians, like the people who started the co-op. They were lumbermen and miners and farmers from around here. They wanted to have their own co-op store, to have shares in it, to

get fair prices. That's what my dad says. He is the manager.

Janko is the butcher. He is left-handed. Mischa is the driver. He delivers the groceries. Aura is the cashier, and Irja is the head clerk.

Sometimes Aura lets me pull the lever that sends the little wooden buckets out to the clerks behind the counters. The buckets move on double wires to whiz the money from the clerks to Aura. They move fast if you pull hard – so I do. And the receipt goes back in a second.

I come straight to the co-op from school today. I want to use the adding machine for my arithmetic homework.

I go up to Aura's office. She smiles and says, "Sure, you can use the adding machine." But before I can start, a man comes to see Aura. I know Mr. Puro, so I say hello.

Aura stops smiling. She says, "I'll see you tomorrow, Kaarina."

I am surprised, but I gather up my books and leave. I wonder what I did wrong?

I decide to give Aura another chance. I go to see

her the next day. Aura smiles and says, "Hello, Sunshine."

I ask her. She says, "Mr. Puro is a board member. He is very strict. He wouldn't like children to be using valuable co-op property. So," she says, "I had to tell you to leave."

It's nice to know that we are still friends. And today I am trying out the adding machine. Aura trusts me to be careful.

Memory Gems and Spelling Bees

I like going to school. I like reading and writing. But not arithmetic.

I know it's good to know how to add and subtract, maybe even do fractions. But it's not as much fun as geography and history and literature. They are about people and places, that's why.

We have to learn memory gems from our primer every week. Memory gems are little poems. I bring them home and read them to Mother. We learn them together.

Mother writes poems herself. She writes them in Finnish, and sometimes she translates English poems into Finnish, too. Maybe one day she will translate one of my memory gems.

She says that some poems move her. She says that they make her feel happy or sad, the way the poet felt when she wrote them. Mother recites them so dramatically that I begin to feel how the poet felt, too.

The most fun, though, are the spelling bees that we have once in awhile. There are two more girls than boys in my class, so sometimes I volunteer to be on the boys' side.

The boys' team wins today's spelling bee, because I am the last one up, and I know how to spell imagination. But even though I am on the boys' team, I am a girl, so I think that the girls are the real winners.

Going to School

This is The Boy's first year at school. Some days he says, "I'll go to school tomorrow." Mother worries that he might find something better to do on the way and not get to school at all. Since one day is as good as another to The Boy, I have to make sure that he gets there, but he walks home with his friends. I do as I please.

The Boy has got his wish to go to school "tomorrow." All the children have the measles except The Boy and me. Even some of the teachers have them.

School is closed for two weeks, and we have a holiday. It's sort of lonely making snowmen by ourselves. I miss my friends, Brownie and Pinkie, the twins who live on the next street. I can only go over and wave to them at their bedroom window.

Now the "holiday" is over. I am so glad to be going to school again. There is only one thing that bothers me about it, and that's Primo.

Primo is a big boy in my class. He likes to pick on the smaller children. He used to punch the boys. Now he is hitting the girls.

A few days ago he kicked my bottom when I didn't notice him behind me. It hurt like anything. Now he catches me and pushes my face down in the snow. I cry and run home.

Mother asks, "What happened to your face? It's all red and wet." I finally tell her all about Primo and the smaller children. She is very angry about it, and tells my dad.

Primo doesn't beat up on us anymore. I think it's because my dad went to Primo's dad and talked to him about it.

Sometimes parents help to solve our worst problems.

Mother Goes to School

The Boy and I leave early to go to school. It's a long walk. We cross the railway tracks at the station and go past the water tower. Water is still dripping from the funnel. A freight engine has just filled up with water.

The Boy stops under the drip, puts his head back and opens his mouth. He says it tastes better than the water from our tap.

We go past the co-op store where Dad works. He waves to us from the front window. We wave back.

Then we climb the long hill to school. The Boy drags his feet, but he always gets to the top sooner than I do. I wonder if he knows the story about the tortoise and the hare?

Mother is coming to school today. She has made an appointment with the Principal, but not about The Boy or me.

The women at the Hall had a meeting. They elected Mother to go to the school with a demand: that the children be allowed to go to the lavatory when they need to. Too many of them go home with wet pants.

So Mother comes to talk with Mr. McGillvary, the Principal. He's the only one who can change the rule.

When we come home for dinner, Mother is smiling. She convinced the Principal to allow the children to go to the lavatory when they have to go. Now we won't have to squirm and wait until recess anymore. How can anybody concentrate on reading or writing if they have to go?

Frances is Shy

Brownie's and Pinkie's dad is a fur trapper's agent.
Indians live on the reservation outside our town.
They sell their pelts to Mr. Sanderson.

A few of the Finnish men we know are
married to Indian women. They don't live on
the reservation. Their children come to our
school. The others call them half-breeds, but
Mother says they are Métis, and just as good as
anybody else.

Frances' dad is Finnish. Her mother is Indian.
She is in my class. She is a quiet girl. She never
answers any of the teacher's questions.

Mother says that Frances is just shy. Sometimes
on Saturday mornings Frances comes to our house to
play with me, but she doesn't talk much. It's hard to
have an interesting conversation with a person who
doesn't talk. But Mother says we need to have all
kinds of friends. Not only the Finns at the Hall, not

only our neighbours, but others who may be different from us.

After lunch one Saturday I walk part way home with Frances. On the way back I stop at Brownie's and Pinkie's house.

Pinkie never stops talking. Brownie never stops giggling. It's fun to be with them, but I keep thinking of Frances. I wonder why she is so quiet. Maybe she just doesn't have anything to say. Maybe she thinks all the time. Maybe she knows how things go without talking about them. Maybe she is just wanting to be quiet and listen to the birds and the trees and the wind.

A Thief in the Night

Mother and Dad like to play bridge. They often play with Pinkie's and Brownie's parents. On Friday night The Boy and I go with them to the Sanderson's house. We play with the twins.

Their bedroom is upstairs. We go up there to see what games we can play when one person is younger than the other three. We choose a jigsaw puzzle. We can talk about anything we want and still play the game.

The Boy gets tired of all those small pieces that look the same and don't fit right. So he goes off to play with the kaleidoscope and listen to the radio. He doesn't tease us at all this time.

Mother calls up to say that they are ready to go home. We go downstairs. I start putting on my coat. Mother asks, "Don't you want to stay overnight with the girls?"

I get a funny feeling. I say, "No, not tonight."

Brownie and Pinkie ask me to stay: "Aw, please stay." But I feel that I just can't. I put on my overshoes, too. I take The Boy's hand and he doesn't object.

Early in the morning the twins come over to our house. They are all excited.

"Someone got into our house last night! He came through the back porch and took our leftover turkey from the food safe. He sure must have been hungry!"

The girls wish I had been there. "A real thief in our house! And you went home," they say.

Yes, it sounds exciting to tell everyone about the thief. But maybe that's why I came home. Maybe I felt that something unusual was going to happen – and it was better to be home safe and sound.

Gymnastics

This is the men's day for gym at the Hall, and Mother and The Boy and I are going to watch.

The Hall is where we meet our friends. We all take part in gymnastics and concerts, dances and plays. Sometimes we are the performers, sometimes we are the audience. Dad says that there are about 50 Finnish Halls all over the country. No matter where we visit, we can go to the Hall. The people we meet there will be friends.

The men are beginning their gymnastics. They leap over the leather horse, they tumble on the mats on the floor and they spin in the air, holding onto the metal rings that hang from the ceiling. They are having a lot of fun!

When the men finish practising I want to try the rings. Mother says they are too high. "If you fall you will hurt yourself," she says. She will not help me to hurt myself.

So I get one of the men to lift me up to grasp the rings. I start swinging, but I am not strong enough to hang on for long. There is nobody there to catch me when I finally have to let go of the rings.

I fall with a thud onto the mats below, knocking the wind out of my lungs. I get scared when I can't catch my breath.

But I get no sympathy from Mother. She just says, "You will be all right soon. That's what you get when you don't do as you're told."

Well, I do catch my breath finally. And I decide then and there that I will learn to do stunts on the rings. I'll show Mother that I can spin in the air just like the men, even if it takes me till next summer.

Children's Gym at the Hall

We go to the Hall every Saturday morning for gym. The Boy is with the other boys at one end, for work on the horse and the mats. I'm at the other end with the girls, for standing exercises. It's fun to do exercises. They make my blood sing and my body feels happy.

Our teachers were trained as gymnasts in Finland. They look professional, even though they are just dads and mothers, like mine. They show us how to bend and stretch properly. They come around and help us move our arms and legs just so.

The first thing I had to learn was telling my left foot from my right. (We always march on stage to perform at our monthly Sunday afternoon concerts, and we all have to be in step.)

The girls wear blue gym bloomers and white shirts. Just like the Finnish flag!

Now we start our exercises: legs apart, arms

extended, bodies bending from the waist to touch our toes. Aili's mother plays the piano; we keep time to the music and do the movements together.

Suddenly as I bend over I fart. Oh, gosh! Nobody could possibly mistake the noise or who made it. I am so embarrassed. I gasp and blush and feel so bad. How could my body do this to me?

But it is funny, too. Everybody laughs, especially the boys. All I can do is laugh with them, just like we do at home. And isn't the Hall our second home? Nobody cares about a little fart. Nobody remembers it the next day. It is just one of those things that happen.

Our Dog Rex

Rex comes to us in a large wooden box. Dad goes to the station to get him.

Dad brings the box home and puts it in the back-yard. He opens one side of it, but the puppy sitting at the back refuses to come out. For about a week Rex stays in the box. Dad puts food and water on the ground just outside the box. Rex eats and drinks when we all go away.

Dad goes to talk to Rex every morning before he walks to work. He doesn't try to get him out of the box.

But this morning, Rex wags his tail a little. Soon he comes to the edge of the box. He sniffs Dad's hand.

Now Rex feels he can trust him, and comes out to investigate the yard.

The Boy and I are impatient. We want to play with our new pet, but Dad says, "We have to let him

get used to us. We are strangers to him. He had to leave his mother and his first home to come to us."

We know that we love Rex already. He is a handsome dog. I wonder when he will get used to us? Will he get used to Missu, too?

Today Dad calls Rex into the house. Rex hesitates, but he trusts Dad now, so he comes in the back door. Missu, our fluffy white cat, comes into the kitchen to see what's up. When she sees Rex, she arches her back and hisses. Rex backs up and looks startled.

Missu spits at him, jumps at his face and scratches his nose. He yips and bats it with his paw. He backs up fast and overturns a chair. He turns around and bumps into the open door, then he sees the way out and runs. Rex is a big puppy. He knows he can't attack a little cat, so all he can do is get away from her.

Now Rex has been with us for the whole summer. He goes everywhere with the family. He goes downtown with Mother to buy bones at the butcher shop. People admire him. I think he likes that!

Mother doesn't worry about The Boy playing outside when Rex is there. He has decided that The Boy is his special responsibility. He knows that The Boy is a rascal and has to be looked after.

Rex lets me pat him and hug him. But Missu sleeps on my bed – alone.

Hoboes in our Town

Our town is bisected by the railroad. That means that it goes right through the middle of town. We live at the far end of the southern half, and our school is away up on a hill on the other side.

The trains rumble past our house. A freight train slows down at our house every morning at eight o'clock. It stops at the station for water. We start for school when it moves on.

All the trains that travel across Canada go right past our door. The hoboes ride on the freight trains.

Hoboes are men and women who are looking for work. They hide in the freight cars because they have no money to pay for a ticket. They stop where they think they might get a job or a meal. People call it riding the rails.

Our house is at the end of Main Street, which runs alongside the railroad tracks. The street has to end there because it meets a huge gully that dips

down to a small stream. It's a favourite spot for the hoboes to make camp. Sometimes we see the glow of their fires at night.

Every time a bunch of hoboes jump off the moving freights, they hurry down into the gully. The CNR police don't like them riding free, so they get off before the train stops at the station. That way, the police don't get the chance to chase them.

Sometimes the hoboes call out hello to The Boy and me when we come home from school. Mother makes sandwiches for the ones who come to our door. She says they are unfortunate people, who want to work, but there are no jobs for them. "We have to share our food with them. We are lucky that Dad has a job," she says.

Our Hall is open to the hoboes, even if they are not Finns. They sleep on the mats we use for tumbling. There is a kitchen at the Hall. There is always stew for the hoboes to eat, simmering in the big kettle.

Some of the hoboes chop wood for the kitchen stove. Dad says, "That's how they thank us. They are good people."

Planting Trees

Our school is having a tree-planting ceremony soon. Every spring we plant a few baby trees. They will get used to their new home during the summer. Then they will be strong enough to survive next winter's storms.

The teacher says that someone from our class should recite a poem at the tree-planting. She asks me if I would like to find a poem and learn it by heart.

I choose *Trees* by Joyce Kilmer. It starts like this:

> I think that I will never see
> A poem lovely as a tree

Mother and I learn it together. We think about the poet's feelings, and we feel the beauty of the trees, too.

At the ceremony, the Principal makes a speech about nature. He says that nature teaches us to appreciate beauty.

When I recite the poem, I feel scared and happy at the same time – and I'm glad when it's over.

I tell Mother and Dad about the tree-planting. Dad says that trees are important to everybody. They are beautiful, but they are useful, too. We heat our houses with wood. We make paper from wood pulp.

Many of our friends are lumbermen. They work hard and long all through the winter, Dad says.

Today Dad comes home with terrible news. The bodies of two Finnish lumber workers have been found after spring thaw. They were shot dead, and their bodies froze near a bush road.

Rosvall and Voutilainen were lumber union organizers. They wanted the lumbermen to join the union, to make working conditions better for them all, the way the union organizers in Finland did. Dad says that there were unions in Finland by 1900, and the Finns who came to Canada brought their union ideas with them.

We all go to the Hall for a memorial meeting for our dead friends. Remembering them, people say they were good, honest men. They tried to help lumber workers get a better life. Is that a reason to kill them?

I go home wondering about life. Beautiful trees and good men cut down. For what?

Mother's Birthday

Mother's favourite time of the year is when the tulips and daffodils bloom. That's when she was born: in April.

This year The Boy and I decide to get flowers. Her birthday falls on Sunday, so we have to buy the flowers on Saturday.

Dad says he will dip into the family's birthday fund to help pay for the flowers. The Boy and I use up our savings.

What to do? How to smuggle flowers into the house without Mother noticing? Where to keep them overnight? We want to surprise her, but we don't have any cubbyholes that she doesn't know about.

On Saturday, Mother goes to choir rehearsal at the Hall, so we go to buy the flowers. We choose the florist's special spring bouquet that has iris in it, too. The flowers come in a long, flat box, just the right size to fit under my bed.

I have to remind The Boy many times that he cannot tell Mother where the flowers are hidden. By the time she comes home, he has stopped wriggling. He plays with his Tinker Toys until bedtime, and keeps our secret.

In the morning, The Boy rushes into my room long before breakfast. He hops and skips around until I get the flower box out from under the bed.

Then we go into Mother's and Dad's bedroom, both holding onto the box. We sing Happy Birthday, and Mother looks pleased. She opens the box and praises the flowers, even though they look a bit wilted. She says, "They are my favourites!" She hugs and kisses us both.

The Boy glows with triumph and tells Mother how I went with him to buy the flowers.

I know it's all right for him to show off, because he is just a little guy. Mother knows that I really managed the whole thing.

Seeds into Flowers

Summer holidays start on the last day of June. The teacher gives us packets of seeds to plant, and I choose bachelor's buttons.

Mother lets me pick a spot in the front yard for my garden. I turn the soil with my garden fork. I add some sheep manure and plant the seeds two inches apart. Then I fill a pail with water and lug it out of the basement to water my garden. I ask the sun to shine so that the seeds will grow!

Finally, after days and days, I see a few green sprouts. Mother says that I must let all the seedlings grow for a few weeks. "You don't want to weed the flower bed too soon. You might pull out the seedlings and leave the weedlings to grow," she laughs.

So I try to learn patience while I give the seeds a chance to grow.

Today, Mother asks me to wash my hands and

face and put on my hat. She and I are going to the Maki's.

Kirsti died yesterday. Mother wants us to visit her mother. Kirsti was just a little girl, who slept in her carriage when her parents brought her to the Hall. Mother says, "She will never come to the Hall again," and her voice sounds strange.

At the house we knock and Kirsti's mother lets us in. She is crying. Mother hugs her.

We go into the front room. There is a little coffin on the table. As I go closer I see Kirsti there in her pretty summer dress, lying with her eyes closed. She is so little and pale and still.

Kirsti is the first dead person I have ever seen. I close my eyes because I don't want to see her dead. I feel as if my chest will burst open.

I run out to the back stoop and cry and cry. I feel as though I can never be happy again.

Mother comes out and finds me. She sits beside me and takes me into her lap. She says quietly, "It is a very sad time for everyone who knew Kirsti. It is sad when loved ones die." Then she takes me by the hand and we walk home together. I feel glad that we are alive.

By August my bachelor's buttons are as tall as The Boy. They are so beautiful that they make my eyes smile when I see them waving in the wind. I don't let anyone cut them. I want them all to live as long as they can.

But I do take some to Kirsti's mother. I want her to have some of the flowers Kirsti did not see.

Saturday Night Sauna

"Finns are so clean," my teacher says. She embarrasses me right in front of the whole class. At least she doesn't say "that's why they are so blonde." Anyway my hair is brown, like Mother's and Dad's, so she can't say that.

Of course, she is right: we are clean. And that's because we go to the sauna. Mother says that taking a sauna bath is the only way to get really clean. Finns invented the sauna, she says. We take baths in our bath tub at home, but every Saturday night we go to the big sauna that the Nurmis run.

There are family and single rooms. Dad buys a family ticket and we go to our dressing room. We all undress. We put our dirty clothes in the bag that Mother brought our clean clothes in.

We go into the bathing room. We each fill a pail with cool water, and then go into the sauna room, climbing up to the highest bench. The higher you go the hotter it is.

Dad throws some water on the hot stones that sit on top of the fire box. The stones sizzle and the hot air rises to warm us up.

The Boy blows on my arm and makes it burn, so I blow on his back and he starts to cry.

Mother moves between us.

We sit in the heat for awhile. We begin to sweat. Then we dip sheaves of birch twigs in our pails of water and smack our bodies with them to make our blood circulate faster. The birch leaves smell fresh and pungent.

In a few minutes we go into the bathing room to wash. We fill our pails with warm water, and really scrub ourselves. I wash The Boy's back and he washes mine, Mother scrubs Dad's back and he scrubs hers.

The Boy and I jump into the big bathtub that's full of cool water. It feels so good to cool down after the hot sauna.

We splash about for awhile, waiting for Mother and Dad to take another turn in the sauna. Then we go into the dressing room to dry our hair and really cool off.

When we're dressed we walk home. I hold Dad's hand, Mother takes The Boy's. It's a lazy walk. We all feel relaxed, but energetic at the same time.

I always sleep soundly on Saturday night. I feel as though I've been washed inside and out – and when I wake up I'm ready for the new day.

Finnish School and Skating

Every Sunday morning at ten o'clock I go to Finnish school at the Hall. I'm learning to read Finnish.

I have an ABC with a red rooster on the cover. The alphabet is the same as in English, but there are two extra letters after z: ä and ö. Each letter sounds exactly the same every time you say it. It's easy to read Finnish.

Only, the words can be hard because I've never heard some of them before, even though we mostly speak Finnish at home. Mother says that it's good to know another language, not just English. She says that learning never lands you in the ditch. That's a funny old Finnish saying.

I guess that's why we speak only Finnish on Wednesdays. Mother won't answer if we speak English. It's frustrating on those days if I forget a Finnish word – just the one I need to tell her something important!

Now I can write to my grandma. She reads Finnish better than English. I can tell her about school and skiing and skating.

Grandma told me that she could ski before she could walk. That's a joke, of course, because skiing is just walking with skis strapped to your feet.

Sometimes we go skating on Sunday afternoons. The Boy wears bob skates over his felt boots. My skates are a bit too big for me, because Mother says they have to last at least two years. We all join hands and glide across the frozen lake. Dad pulls us. The Boy is at the end as Dad "cracks the whip." The Boy lets go and flies over the ice – "Whee!"

Yes, Grandma will be happy to get my letters. She likes people to have fun.

Sunday Dinner

We always have dinner at noon. That's our biggest meal of the day. We have time to enjoy it, because school begins again at one-thirty.

Herring casserole is my favourite. Mother says it's like scalloped potatoes but with layers of salt herring between the layers of sliced potatoes and onions.

I try not to bite the allspice peppers. They are bitter. But Mother says that they flavour the casserole. The butter she puts on top makes it taste scrumptious. Mmm!

Sometimes we go to the Finnish boarding house for Sunday dinner. Mother says that the cook at our house needs a day off once in awhile.

The dining room has three long tables covered with oilcloth, with benches on either side. We sit in a row. I sit beside Dad.

There are bowls and platters and baskets full of

food. We can fill our plates as often as we like. Hardtack and fresh rye bread (no white bread here) are in the baskets. Liver pudding, meat balls, herring casserole, and root vegetable salad are in the bowls and platters.

The Boy and I keep an eye on the desserts: rice pudding, prune whip, raisin pie. I guess I don't have a favourite. I just like them all.

Meals at the boarding house for our family cost $3, $1.25 each for Mother and Dad, and 25¢ each for The Boy and me. I would have to save my allowance for over a year to treat my family to a meal here!

Dad Loses His Job

A terrible thing has happened. Dad lost his job. It's because of the Depression.

Mother and Dad decide that we have to go to live with my grandparents.

We drive hundreds of miles in our old Essex. The Boy and I sleep off and on in the back seat, but it feels like forever before we arrive.

Now we get to our grandparents' house. And everybody hugs and kisses everybody else.

There are lots of bedrooms in their house, but my grandparents have two roomers. It's because of the Depression. So I have to share with The Boy. We have our own beds, but it's not the same as having your own room.

The Boy and I go to King Edward Public School. That's the school my mother went to when she first came from Finland. She says that it was strange to be the biggest girl in the class, and the only one who didn't know how to speak English, but she learned quickly.

Now my new teacher says that I have to catch up in arithmetic. The teacher at home hadn't taught us fractions before I left my old school. But now I have to learn them, because everybody else can do the problems. And I can't.

When she says this I feel so bad that I just leave school and run home. But when I get there, the house is empty.

So I run down the street. I keep calling, Dad! Dad! as I run.

Then a car stops near me and Dad jumps out. He holds out his arms. I run into them and cry and cry.

He takes me home. I tell him about the fractions. He says, "We'll just take your arithmetic book out right now and see what we can do."

He explains fractions to me. I do a few problems. They are not so hard.

Today I take a note to the teacher saying that I was not very well yesterday. It is signed by Dad. And when we do fractions, I only make two mistakes.

Candies and Shinplasters

Mother gives me a shinplaster. It's for a pound of hamburg from Kallio's butcher shop. We're going to have meat balls for dinner.

I skip up the street to The Hill. That's where the first Finns settled in the city. Most of the stores at The Hill are owned by Finns.

There is no hill at The Hill, though. When I ask Grandpa where the hill is, he just laughs. Mother says that it's just a name. I keep wondering why The Hill is not a hill.

First I come to Konka's shoe repair shop. Allan Konka is a friend of The Boy's. They're the same age.

The Boy was playing with Allan the day he broke his arm. Dr. Hänninen, right next door, set The Boy's arm and put a cast on it. The Boy wasn't a bit scared, because Dr. Hänninen is a good friend of his.

The Boy had to wear the cast for three weeks.

He would swing his arm-in-the-cast around and around. Everybody had to jump out of his way.

He couldn't go to the sauna. If he did, the heat would melt the cast and the sweat would tickle his arm.

I'm not sure he really wanted to go to the sauna anyway.

Lahti's gas station is on the next corner. That's where Dad gets gas for the Essex.

Now I'm right in the middle of The Hill. I stand here and look around. Almost every store and house I can see belongs to Finns. And they are all friends of mine.

Across the street, Aunt Hanna is calling me. She is not my real aunt. I like to visit her because she lets me have coffee and cake like a grownup. I can never have coffee at home, even with lots of milk in it, like Aunt Hanna gives me – Mother says that coffee is for adults, milk is for children.

I would like to pat Aunt Hanna's cat. Fluffy is a long-haired, striped cat. I call her Tiger to myself. She likes to hide behind Aunt Hanna's ficus and rubber plants. She pounces on me when I come near. But I can't stop to visit Aunt Hanna today.

Now I have to hurry to Kallio's to get the meat for dinner. What was it Mother wanted? Sausages or hamburg?

I ask Mr. Kallio how much sausages cost. He says "Twenty-four cents a pound."

"How much does hamburg cost?"

"Twenty-five cents a pound."

I have a shinplaster. If I get the sausages, there will be one cent left over for my trouble. If I get the hamburg, I won't be able to get a licorice pipe.

What a problem!

Well, one cent is not very much. But a licorice pipe is a treat. And don't I deserve a treat?

Mother doesn't think so. She is waiting for me when I come home. When she sees the sausages she gets angry. Then I remember that she wanted hamburg. Oh, oh!

Well, I suppose that I am lucky Mother didn't make me stay home from Saturday gym at the Hall. But she docked one cent from my five-cent weekly allowance for three weeks.

I suppose you have to pay for your mistakes.

At the Hall

I am glad that there is a Finnish Hall in this town.
Grandma is there this afternoon, rehearsing a play.
Soon we will go to the first night.

Grandma was an actress at the Tampere
Workers' Theatre in Finland. She worked during the
day in a textile factory. At night she went to the
theatre to rehearse her role in the plays or to sing in
the choir.

Once, when we were here on a visit and The
Boy was a lot smaller than he is now, we all went to
the Hall to see one of Grandma's plays.

All the children sat down in the front row.
Grandma came on stage all dressed up like a queen.
The Boy ran up to the stage! He pointed and said in
a loud voice, "That's my grandma." I rushed to
bring him back to his seat. Everybody knows that's
our grandma!

Mother and Grandma sing in the women's choir.

Grandma sings soprano; Mother sings alto. They harmonize so beautifully. When I get bigger I'm going to sing like an angel, and be in the choir, too.

Mother says that she was teaching a Finnish folk dance to the little girls at the Hall just the day before I was born. Imagine, I learned to dance in my mother's womb! Maybe that's why I like dancing so much. I dance in the folk dancing group and I know three dances already.

The Boy and I sing on stage at this Sunday's concert. Mother says we are singing for friends, so we needn't have stage fright.

We hold hands and stand close together. The Boy is a happy-go-lucky little guy; he doesn't care if his socks are at half-mast.

Well, I do. But it's too late to pull them up when we are already on stage.

Afterwards, Grandma and Grandpa congratulate us. Other people pat our heads and smile. Mother tells us that older people enjoy seeing children perform. That makes us feel good! The Boy and I decide to learn another song to sing at the next concert.

Learning to Knit

Mother says, "You'll never marry a rich man, so you'd better learn to cook and knit and sew."

It's fun learning to cook and knit and sew. I don't care if I never marry anybody.

Mother is even more impatient than I am. That's why Grandma says *she* will teach me to knit.

Christmas is coming, and I want to knit a pot holder for my aunt. The first thing is to cast on 30 stitches.

"You cast them on onto two needles held together, so that the bottom edge will be loose and springy," Grandma says.

She is teaching me the Finnish way to knit. She says it's different from the English way, and faster.

"Knitting isn't too hard," she says. "There are only two basic stitches to learn, knit and purl." Once I learn the knit stitch, she says to keep on doing them to the end of the row, then do the same thing from the beginning of each new row.

Soon I have knitted four rows. I count the stitches to make sure there are still 30.

Oh, no! There are only 29. Where is the 30th stitch?

Grandma comes to my rescue. She says I dropped one stitch, but she soon finds it and picks it up. She says I have to learn a few tricks like picking up dropped stitches. "It's not *all* just knit and purl," she says. "You will learn the tricks as you go."

Already it's bedtime, and I've only knitted seven rows. I wonder how long it will take to knit this pot holder?

Maybe I'd better marry a rich man, after all!

My Cousin My Sister

My cousin Helena is a little older than The Boy, and
a little younger than I am, so she could be our sister.
We're lucky she is our cousin. When she comes to
visit us with my Aunt Kaarina, they sometimes stay
a whole week.

It's fun to have company. Mother and Aunt and
Grandma talk and talk. Sometimes they sing
together, like in the choir, and we all join in.

Helena is an only child. She only has a dog
called Blackie to love. Brothers are better.

On the last visit, Helena told me that her mother
wants her to be perfect. When she comes second in
class, Aunt Kaarina asks her why she didn't come
first. It made her feel like not working so hard all the
time, so she didn't any more.

Then her marks went down. Her mother got
angry, and the Principal called Helena into his office.

They had a talk about smart Finns. He said,

"You are one of them, Helena. But you have to do some work to show that you are smart." He asked her why she didn't want to work harder. She told him that she used to try hard, but it never seemed good enough.

They had a few more talks after that, and Helena said that the Principal seemed to understand. He reminded her that the teacher thinks well of her, and she started to feel better. She decided that maybe she ought to try harder. She wants to show the Principal that she is as smart as he knows she can be.

Helena's coming to visit us by herself for the summer holidays! Maybe Aunt Kaarina has decided to let Helen visit us as a reward for working so hard.

The Three-Nickel Day

Mother gave me my allowance today. It's not just the usual nickel, but a special one – a great big American buffalo nickel. She says, "You should leave it at home. It will burn a hole in your pocket until you spend it!" I leave it in my secret hiding place under the loose floorboard in Grandma's room.

Mother says that I may visit Grandpa at his shop after school. Jane comes with me. She's in my class.

Grandpa's shop has a black and gold sign in the window. It says, H.E. Heinonen, Tailor. It's been there since 1912, when he arrived from Finland.

Grandpa works alone now, but eight tailors worked in his shop before the Depression. They all came from Finland, too. They had their journey-man's papers that say they are professional tailors, just like my Grandpa. Nowadays people are too poor to buy tailor-made clothes, so there was not enough work for all those tailors, and he had to let them go. He must have hated doing that.

When we come into the shop, Grandpa is sitting cross-legged on the heavy wooden cutting table. He is mending a coat. His round spectacles sit on the middle of his nose. He glances over the rims and sees me. He says, "What a surprise, to see my favourite granddaughter here."

I tell him that my friend Jane and I came straight from school.

Grandpa lifts us up beside him. He gives me a hug and chucks Jane under the chin. We swing our legs. Then he says,

"Maybe you want a little something on the way home. Here's a nickel, Kaarina. Buy some candy for Jane, too." I wrap the nickel up in my hanky and put it in my pocket. I say thank you, and we all say goodbye.

Outside, Jane says that Grandpa speaks funny English. It makes me feel kind of strange that she said that. Grandpa's English is okay, only he speaks with a Finnish accent. Anyway, most of the time he speaks Finnish, because most of his customers do.

We skip along to the corner and I turn and look back. Grandpa is there, waving, and I wave too.

We go down to Kivi's grocery store. Mr. Kivi has cent candies, and the licorice comes right from Finland. Jane and I look over the whole window of candies, and decide on licorice pipes and black balls and caramels.

We go in. I dig in my pocket for the nickel Grandpa gave me. I pull out my hanky and open it up. The nickel is not there.

I put my hand into my pocket again, but it's not there, for sure. Jane puts her hand in, but she can't find it, either. It sure has burnt a hole in my pocket, this time.

We leave without the "little something" Grandpa wanted us to have.

We cross the street. A big green wooden streetcar clangs to a stop. The men getting off carry empty dinner pails. It must be late.

We race off home. I run up the verandah steps and look through the lace curtains at the oval window in the door. I can see Grandma at the kitchen table. She is singing as she works.

Grandma says that I am the first one home, so I tell her about my disappointment.

She says, "Never mind, you still have your allowance." And I had forgotten all about it!

I run upstairs to Grandma's bedroom. I lift the loose floorboard and feel around for my buffalo nickel. I find a nickel, but it's not the buffalo nickel that Mother gave me. So I feel around some more. My fingers touch another coin. This is the right one. Now I have two nickels!

So it's just as though I hadn't lost Grandpa's nickel, after all. And tomorrow I can treat Jane.

Moving On

It's funny how things can change so fast, in just a few minutes. Yesterday was the same as the day before. Today everything is different.

Today Dad got a very important letter. It says he has a new job at a dairy co-op up north. He will be the manager.

The whole family is buzzing with this good news. And people are saying that the Depression is really over now. Hoboes will not have to be hoboes anymore. They will not have to ride the rails. They will have jobs and homes. And enough to eat.

Grandpa and Dad will not have to go hunting for deer, either, like they did last winter when the shop wasn't doing well.

But we have just got settled at Grandma's and Grandpa's house. The Boy and I even divided our bedroom to suit us both, and we don't ever need to step over the dividing line to find our own things.

We like this house. We've got lots of room to play in the verandah behind the kitchen. We know which steps creak on the way upstairs. And we have our very own hidey-holes. Now we will have to get used to another house. The Boy and I don't want to move.

We tell Mother and Dad that we don't want to move again. Mother says, "We'll have to have a family discussion about that." We tell them why we don't want to leave. Then Dad says, "I can understand how you feel, but it is very important for me to have a job. I have to support the family, and the Depression used up all our savings. We have to move."

The Boy and I look at one another. Now we can understand why we have to go. The next day, we start packing, too.

Mother and Dad are very busy. They have brought the trunks up from the basement and they sort things from morning to night.

There is a wooden butter-box for The Boy's toys and treasures; mine go into an apple storage basket. It has a round wooden cover. I'm going to keep it forever, it pleases me so much.

Moving day is getting closer. When I think of leaving Grandma and Grandpa, I get a little frightened and I cry.

But Grandma hugs me and says that they will come to visit us when we get settled. That makes me feel better. Still, I will miss her hugs at home and her majesty on the stage. And I won't be able to visit Grandpa at his tailor shop anymore.

Our friends from the Hall come to say farewell. They tell us that we will meet again at the Finnish Summer Festival next year and every year after that. So we will keep our friends, even if we don't see them very often.

Mother and Dad are happy to be moving. They talk about the new house waiting for us, and the new school where The Boy and I will go. And Dad's important new job.

This move will be a whole new adventure for all of us, Mother says.

Now we are ready. The moving van has come and gone. The old Essex is full of gas and ready to go.

We have one more dinner together at the

big round dining room table. Everyone is excited and happy.

Then Mother says, "It's time to go. Have you remembered to pack everything?"

I run upstairs one more time. I go to Grandma's bedroom. I lift the loose floorboard once more, just to make sure that there are no more nickels hidden there.

I wonder whether there is a loose floorboard somewhere in our new house?

I run downstairs again. Everyone is hugging and kissing everyone else, just like when we moved here last year.

Even if we don't live in their house, our grandparents will always be our grandparents. They will always love us. And we will love them.

We can say goodbye. And not cry.

We are all ready for our new adventure now.

GLOSSARY OF UNFAMILIAR WORDS

Allspice Peppers – Also known as allspice berries. They are the dried seeds of the allspice tree, and are used in cooking and baking.

Bob Skates – Skates having two parallel blades.

Buffalo Nickel – An American nickel that had an impression of a buffalo on one side.

Butter-box – A wooden box, about 2' × 2', lined with wax and used for the storage of butter.

Chipso – A brand of laundry soap used in the 1930s.

Depression – A term referring to the state of a country's economy. The depression in Kaarina's story, also known as The Great Depression, began with the stock market crash of 1929 and lasted until approximately 1938. Eventually the entire world was affected by it. Banks failed, which meant that people lost all their savings, and millions of people lost their jobs.

Hardtack – Slightly different from the hardtack of pioneer times, the hardtack that the Finns made was made from rye flour and water. It had no raising agent, so it stayed flat, and was baked until very hard. It was round, with a hole in the middle, and quite salty.

Lavatory – The toilet, or the room where the toilet is. This word is still common in the British Isles.

Shinplaster – A small paper note, about $1\frac{1}{2}$" × 3", worth 25¢. It was nicknamed shinplaster because it looked like a plaster, which is another word for a small adhesive bandage.